HERE'S **HEATHCLIFF**

AMERICA'S
CRAZIEST
CAT!

Volume III

© McNaught Synd., Inc.

THE BEST OF SUNDAY WITH HEATHCLIFF

# SPECIALTIES, ON THE HOUSE

A TOM DOHERTY ASSOCIATES BOOK

HEATHCLIFF: SPECIALTIES, ON THE HOUSE
Volume III of HERE'S HEATHCLIFF

Copyright © 1981 by McNaught Syndicate, Inc.

Reprinted by arrangement with Windmill Books, Inc. and Simon and Schuster, a division of Gulf and Western Corp.

A TOR Book

Published by Tom Doherty Associates, Inc.
49 West 24 Street
New York, N.Y. 10010

First Tor printing: September 1985
Second printing: February 1987

ISBN: 0-812-56816-8
CAN. ED.: 0-812-56817-6

Printed in the United States of America

0 9 8 7 6 5 4 3 2

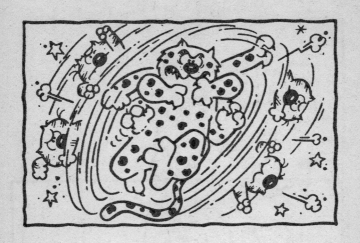

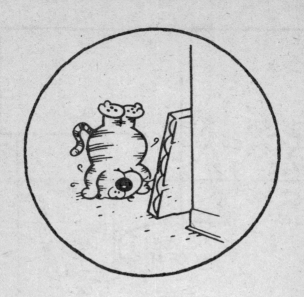

I WANT YOU TO SEE THE PAINTING I'M WORKING ON....

1977
2-27 McNaught Synd., Inc.

# A METHOD TO HIS MADNESS

by Geg Gately

LOOK WHAT GRANDMA BOUGHT YOU!

THUMP-A-THUMP...

# FISHY
# BUSINESS

by Bob Gately

AH, MULCAHY... HOW ARE THINGS GOING?

WE'VE GOT A PROBLEM!

# ADVENTURES OF A WATCHCAT

by Geo Gately

BURGLAR ALARM

THE NUTMEGS

1977
McNaught
Syndicate, Inc.

THE TRANSFORMATION

by Bob Gately

5-8 1977
McNaught
Syndicate, Inc.

5-22   McNaught Synd., Inc.
1977

# A DAY AT THE RACES

by Geo Gately

1977
McNaught
Syndicate. Inc.
5-5

6-5
1977
McNaught Synd., Inc.

# CHAMPIONSHIP
## FORM

by Gately

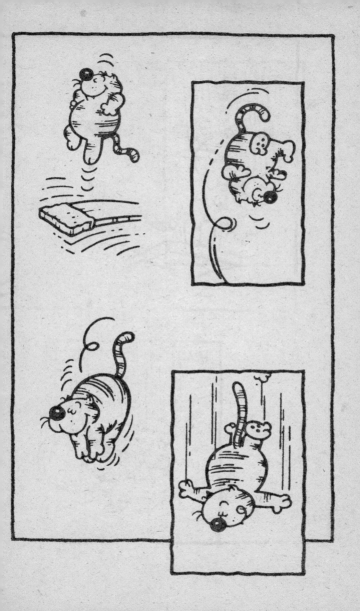

THERE'S HEATHCLIFF, BUT HE WON'T COME IN UNLESS HE'S DRIVEN IN A CART LIKE A MAJOR LEAGUER!

DO YOU HAVE YOUR DOLL CARRIAGE OUT THERE? HOW 'BOUT USING THAT?

7-3  1977
McNaught Synd., Inc.

FUNNY ANIMAL ACTS...

by Geo Gately

ISN'T THAT A GREAT TRAINED DOG ACT?!

YAWN!

1977
McNaught Synd. Inc.

# HEATHCLIFF

## AMERICA'S CRAZIEST CAT

☐ 56800-1  SPECIALTIES ON THE HOUSE  $1.95
   56801-X                    Canada $2.50

☐ 56802-8  HEATHCLIFF AT HOME        $1.95
   56803-6                    Canada $2.50

☐ 56804-4  HEATHCLIFF AND THE        $1.95
   56805-2     GOOD LIFE       Canada $2.50

☐ 56806-0  HEATHCLIFF: ONE, TWO, THREE $1.95
   56807-9     AND YOU'RE OUT  Canada $2.50

Buy them at your local bookstore or use this handy coupon:
Clip and mail this page with your order

---

TOR BOOKS—Reader Service Dept.
49 W. 24 Street, 9th Floor, New York, NY 10010

Please send me the book(s) I have checked above. I am
enclosing $_____ (please add $1.00 to cover postage
and handling). Send check or money order only—
no cash or C.O.D.'s.

Mr./Mrs./Miss _____

Address _____

City _____ State/Zip _____
Please allow six weeks for delivery. Prices subject to
change without notice.

# BEETLE BAILEY
# THE WACKIEST G.I. IN THE ARMY

Buy them at your local bookstore or use this handy coupon:
Clip and mail this page with your order

TOR BOOKS—Reader Service Dept.
49 W. 24 Street, 9th Floor, New York, NY 10010

Please send me the book(s) I have checked above. I am enclosing
$_____ (please add $1.00 to cover postage and handling).
Send check or money order only—no cash or C.O.D.'s.

Mr./Mrs./Miss _____
Address _____
City _____ State/Zip _____
Please allow six weeks for delivery. Prices subject to change without
notice.